A Story for Deb

THE MAN WHO WALKED THE EARTH

IAN WALLACE

A Groundwood Book   Douglas & McIntyre   Toronto Vancouver Berkeley

THE DAY MY FATHER LEFT HOME in search of work, my mother told me to set an extra place at the table in case someone who needed a meal came to the door.

"No one's going to stop here," I told her. "We live in the middle of nowhere."

She looked out the window at the land that lay as flat as a breadboard to the horizon. The wind whipped the dry earth into dust.

"Wherever your father is, I hope someone will set a place for him," she said.

Eight months passed. Almost seven hundred and fifty extra plates for me and twelve odd jobs for my father. Not one stranger stepped onto our land or knocked on our door. And then it happened.

It was Christmas. My sister Elise and I were feeling sad, thinking about our dad and wishing he was home. He hadn't written in three weeks. He'd promised to send presents, but none had arrived. So in the morning when we woke up, there were only two pairs of knitted socks and two boxes of crayons for us under the tree.

Our Christmas dinner was almost eaten – a rabbit my mother had cooked with potatoes, a turnip and carrots from the root cellar – when we suddenly heard a knock on the door.

Elise dropped her fork and I shot straight out of my chair. I threw open the door. In the moonlight, I could see a man as large and woolly as a grizzly.

"Would you have a spare bite for a man who's walked the earth?" he asked.

My mother stood up. "Please come out of the cold and join us, Mr...."

"Balzini. Balzini's my name."

He left his snowshoes on the porch, and my mother hung up his bearskin coat and hat. Then he sat down at the table and ate the last of the vegetables. He even sucked the bones of the rabbit clean.

As he ate, I riddled him with questions about where he'd been.

"Every city and town you can name, boy. Over mountains and through forests. Across rivers and prairies."

"Maybe you ran into my dad. He's working in a sawmill in the Rocky Mountains right now."

The stranger mopped up the last bit of gravy with a slice of bread. "I wish I could say I had."

"That's enough, André," my mother said. "You'll wear Mr. Balzini out with all your questions."

She got up from the table and cleared the dirty plates and cutlery. The stranger, Elise and I sat in awkward silence. I could hear my mother fussing at the kitchen sink and the sound of the wind rattling the windows.

A grin crossed the stranger's face. He unscrewed the lid from the salt shaker and held it up for my sister and me to see. Then he tipped the shaker, pouring the salt into a fist that he made with his left hand.

The clock struck six. He set the shaker down and opened his hand. It was empty. There wasn't a grain of salt to be seen.

We looked at his right hand that was now all clenched up, too. He loosened his fist just a pinch. Out flowed a stream of glistening salt back into the shaker.

My sister squealed with delight while I just stared in amazement. When the shaker was full, he screwed the lid on and sat back in his chair.

"Mama, Mama, Mr. Balzini's a magician," I called out.

"He surely is," she replied from the pantry. "He made a whole plate of food disappear."

"No, Mama," Elise said. "He made the salt disappear and reappear!"

"And I'm going to make your favorite pie appear before your eyes."

"Do the trick again, Mr. Balzini," I begged.

"Yes, do it again," Elise said.

"Hush, now," my mother said as she returned with the apple pie. "And stop pestering our guest."

She cut the pie and gave Mr. Balzini half. Elise and I stared in disbelief. No one ever got half a pie at one sitting in our house. I watched in silent envy as he ate every bit of the crust and every drop of the sweet filling.

"That was one fine meal," he said. "The best I've had in some time."

"I'm pleased we could share it with you," my mother said.

The stranger pushed back his chair. "Now, I must be going. I have a place to sleep tonight and I want to be there before it is too late." He put on his bearskin coat and hat. "Before I do, though, I have a small thank-you for your hospitality."

He reached inside one sleeve, and I heard the sound of Christmas bells. Out came a string of colorful scarves that soared about the room. He gave the scarves to my mother, who lifted them to her nose.

"Told you he was a magician, Mama," I said.

"The scent is lavender. From France," he told her. "And the silk is from China."

"I couldn't accept such a lovely gift. I… " She inhaled deeply. Elise and I scrambled from our chairs to catch the scent, too. It was the most beautiful smell I'd ever known.

Then Mr. Balzini reached inside his coat. "Ta-*da*!" he cheered, as he pulled out a brilliant yellow sunflower. He handed it to Elise. She touched the leaves. "They're real, Mama!"

The stranger tapped a finger against his lip. "Now, one more gift. Let me see. Yes, yes… I've got it."

He let us look inside his bearskin hat. Nothing was there. He tossed the hat up into the air, from one hand to the other. "Reach inside, André."

I pulled out my gift. "*A Boy's Handbook of Magic* by The Great Balzini." I looked up at him. "You *are* a magician."

"André, Elise," he said. "Hold out one hand and make a wish."

Mr. Balzini moved his hands in quick circles. Then he smacked them together and a stream of glistening salt flowed from his left hand, until he had made a pile in each of our palms.

"Shazam, shazam," he said and opened the door. He picked up his snowshoes. "Thank you again. And Merry Christmas."

My mother and Elise looked as if a spell had been cast over them. My feet felt like they were wearing granite shoes. Finally, they grew wings. I flew out the door to see him step into the shadow of the barn.

"Merry Christmas, Mr. Balzini. You're a great magician!"

He waved good-bye, and I tossed the salt into the air. In the blink of an eye the grains sparkled and the sky streaked red. The color was faint at first, but grew more vibrant, rippling in waves like the Northern Lights.

My mother and Elise appeared in the doorway.

"Toss your salt in the air, Elise!"

Her grains sparkled and the color rippled. She clapped her hands in delight, and the color moved to the rhythm. My mother and I joined her and the sky burst into brilliant life over our house.

A warm glow passed through my body, and I didn't feel so alone anymore.

All too soon, the light faded away and was gone. I looked at my hand, almost not believing what had happened.

We returned indoors and sat by the tree we'd chopped down and decorated on Christmas Eve. I read *A Boy's Handbook of Magic* out loud and rubbed away the remaining grains of salt that were stuck between my fingers.

I had just begun Chapter Three, titled "Salt Magic," when there was a knock on the door. My mother, Elise and I looked at one another. Could it be?

"Shazam, shazam." I raced into the kitchen. "Welcome back, Mr. Balzini." I threw the door open.

"Would you have a spare bite for a man who's walked the earth?" I heard.

"Papa," I cried and leapt into his arms. My mother and sister rushed out and joined our embrace. "You're the best wish come true."

We went back indoors. My mother brought my father something to eat. Leftover macaroni and cheese, and a dill pickle. We showed him the gifts Mr. Balzini had given us.

While he ate we told him about the stranger who had come to our table earlier that night, and had left as swiftly as the grains of salt that slipped through his hands.

Copyright © 2003 by Ian Wallace

No part of this publication may be reproduced, stored in a retrieval system or transmitted, in any form or by any means, without the prior written consent of the publisher or a licence from The Canadian Copyright Licensing Agency (Access Copyright). For an Access Copyright licence, visit www.accesscopyright.ca or call toll free to 1-800-893-5777.

Groundwood Books / Douglas & McIntyre
720 Bathurst Street, Suite 500, Toronto, Ontario
Distributed in the USA by Publishers Group West
1700 Fourth Street, Berkeley, CA 94710

We acknowledge for their financial support of our publishing program the Canada Council for the Arts, the Government of Canada through the Book Publishing Industry Development Program (BPIDP), the Ontario Arts Council and the Government of Ontario through the Ontario Media Development Corporation's Ontario Book Initiative.

ONTARIO ARTS COUNCIL
CONSEIL DES ARTS DE L'ONTARIO

National Library of Canada Cataloging in Publication
Wallace, Ian
The man who walked the earth / by Ian Wallace.
ISBN 0-88899-545-8
I. Title.
PS8595.A566M35 2003   jC813'.54   C2003-900370-1
PZ7

Library of Congress Control Number: 2003100266

Printed and bound in China by Everbest Printing Co. Ltd.